My Weirde

Mr. Cooper Is Super!

Dan Gutman

Pictures by
Jim Paillot

HARPER
An Imprint of HarperCollinsPublishers

To Jonathan Streib

My Weirdest School #1: Mr. Cooper Is Super!
Text copyright © 2015 by Dan Gutman
Illustrations copyright © 2015 by Jim Paillot

Library of Congress Cataloging-in-Publication Data

Gutman, Dan.

Mr. Cooper is super! / Dan Gutman ; pictures by Jim Paillot.

pages   cm — (My weirdest school ; 1)

Summary: "A.J. and the gang at Ella Mentry School are in for a super surprise when
a new teacher, Mr. Cooper, takes over their third grade class"— Provided by publisher.

ISBN 978-0-06-228421-1 (pbk. bdg.) — ISBN 978-0-06-228422-8 (lib. bdg.)

[1. Schools—Fiction. 2. Teachers—Fiction. 3. Extraterrestrial beings—Fiction.
4. Unidentified flying objects—Fiction. 5. Humorous stories.] I. Title.

PZ7.G9846Mp 2015   2014022681

[Fic]—dc23   CIP

                                                                          AC

Typography by Aurora Parlagreco
18 19 20   BRR   10
❖
First Edition

Contents

1. Look! Up in the Sky!   1

2. You Should Have Been There!   8

3. Mr. Granite Is from Another Planet   15

4. Saying Good-bye Is Sad   26

5. The New Teacher   39

6. Mr. Cooper Is Super!   48

7. Rat Man   60

8. The Attack of Super Librarian   70

9. The Truth about Mr. Cooper   83

10. The Big Surprise Ending!   95

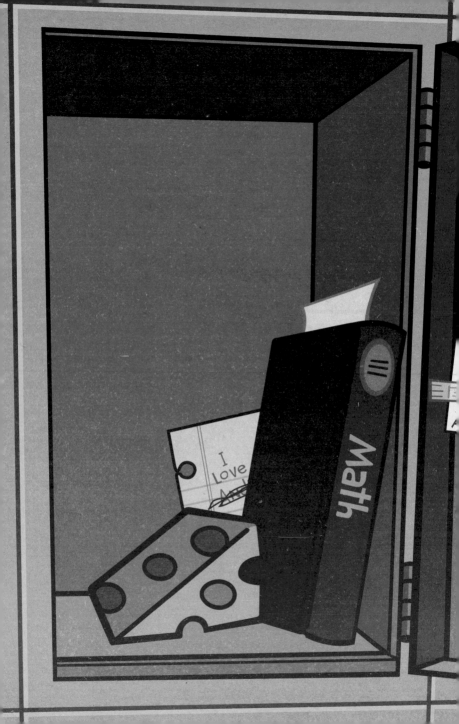

Look! Up in the Sky!

My name is A.J., and I hate it when an alien spaceship lands in the middle of the playground.

You probably think that's some kind of a joke. But it's not. A joke would be, like . . .

Q: Why do seagulls fly over the sea?

A: Because if they flew over the bay, they'd be bagels.

1

Get it? Seagulls? Baygulls? Bagels? Anyway, the point is that it was no joke. The other day at Ella Mentry School, an alien spaceship actually landed in the middle of the playground! For real!

Let me explain. It was right after lunch. Me and the gang were at recess with our teacher, Mr. Granite. I borrowed a football from Michael, who never ties his shoes. I was throwing it back and forth with Ryan,

who will eat anything, even stuff that isn't food. Michael was playing on the monkey bars with Alexia, this girl who rides a skateboard all the time, and Neil, who we call the nude kid even though he wears clothes.

"Hey, A.J.!" Michael shouted. "Give me the football back. It's my turn."

"In a minute!" I hollered. "We're not done yet."

"You should give Michael his ball, Arlo," said Andrea Young, this annoying girl with curly brown hair. She calls me by my real name because she knows I don't like it. "When you borrow something from somebody, you should return it when they ask for it."

"When are you going to return your *face* to the ugly person you borrowed it from?" I asked Andrea.

"Oh, snap!" said Ryan.

"That's mean!" said Emily, Andrea's cry-baby friend.

It was none of Andrea's beeswax. I could tell she was going to say something mean to me, but she didn't get the chance. Because that's when the weirdest thing in the history of the world happened.

"Look! Up in the sky!" shouted Michael.

"It's a bird!" shouted Ryan.

"It's a plane!" shouted Neil the nude kid.

"It's—"

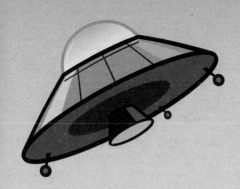

No, actually, it *was* a bird and a plane. You see birds and planes in the sky all the time. What's the big deal? I went back to throwing the football around with Ryan.

But a minute later, I noticed Mr. Granite. He was staring up at the sky. He had a weird expression on his face.

"Look! Up in the sky!" shouted Alexia.

"It's a bird!" shouted Ryan.

"It's a plane!" shouted Neil.

"No, it's a *spaceship*!" shouted Michael.

Yes, it was a spaceship. You probably *still* think I'm making all this up. But it's *true*!

You Should Have Been There!

When Mr. Granite became our third-grade teacher a million hundred months ago, I suspected that he was really an alien from another planet. There were two reasons. First, our principal, Mr. Klutz, told us there was a flying saucer in the teachers'

8

lounge.* Second, I noticed that Mr. Granite didn't have any hair growing out of his nose or ears.

My dad has hair growing out of his nose and ears. He even has this little machine he sticks in his nose and ears every few days so he can give himself a little haircut in there. *All* men have to trim their nose and ear hair. It's the first rule of being a man. But Mr. Granite didn't have any nose or ear hair at *all*. Clearly, he was not from planet Earth.

To see if my theory was right, the gang and me snuck over to Mr. Granite's house

---

*It turned out that the teachers were throwing teacups around.

that day. We were like spies. It was cool. And guess what we saw? Mr. Granite was building a spaceship in his garage! The spaceship was powered by microwaved potatoes. We caught him red-handed.

Mr. Granite admitted to us that he was born on the planet Etinarg, which is "granite" spelled backward. He told us he was planning to blast off and go back to Etinarg the next day. The only problem was that a cow bumped into his spaceship just as it was taking off. Mr. Granite parachuted out before his spaceship exploded, and he was forced to stay on Earth and teach third grade to us. It's a long, sad story.*

So anyway, back to what happened the other day during recess. We were all looking up in the sky. The spaceship was coming down, slowly. It was round and silver and spaceshipy-looking.

"Run for your lives!" shouted Neil the nude kid.

"I'm scared!" said Emily, who is scared of everything.

"This is cool!" I said.

At first I thought that maybe we were just having some kind of a drill. Like, we have fire drills all the time in case there's

---

*And it's called *Mr. Granite Is from Another Planet!* Available at your local bookseller. Order yours today!

11

ever a fire at school. Maybe this was a drill in case there's ever an alien spaceship coming to take over the earth.

But it wasn't a drill. It was the real thing! A spaceship was about to land in the playground. You should have been there! We got to see it live and in person!

Smoke poured out of the spaceship as it hovered over the playground.

Colored lights were flashing.

There was a weird humming sound.
The spaceship touched down gently.

All the smoke and lights and humming stopped.

I looked at Michael. Michael looked at Ryan. Ryan looked at Neil. Neil looked at Alexia. Alexia looked at me. Then we all looked at Mr. Granite. He was staring at the spaceship.

A ramp slid down from the bottom of the ship. And you'll never believe in a million hundred years who walked out.

I'm not going to tell you.

Okay, okay, I'll tell you. But you have to read the next chapter. So nah-nah-nah boo-boo on you.

Mr. Granite Is from Another Planet

It was Mr. Granite!

Well, it wasn't *our* Mr. Granite, because he was standing right next to us. But the alien who came down the ramp of the spaceship looked *just* like Mr. Granite!

Our teacher Mr. Granite just stood there with a look of wonder on his face.

"Who are you?" we all asked the alien who looked just like Mr. Granite.

"I am Mr. Granite," said the alien.

"You can't be Mr. Granite!" said Andrea. "Mr. Granite is our teacher, and he's standing right here."

"I am Mr. Granite," repeated the alien who looked just like Mr. Granite.

And you'll never believe in a million hundred years what happened next.

Ten *more* aliens climbed out of the spaceship and came down the ramp. And every one of them looked just like Mr. Granite!

"Who are *you* guys?" we all asked.

"I am Mr. Granite."

"I am Mr. Granite."

"I am Mr. Granite."

"I am Mr. Granite."

In case you were wondering, all the aliens were saying, "I am Mr. Granite." That was weird.

"Will the real Mr. Granite please stand up?" I asked.

"They're *all* the real Mr. Granite," said our teacher Mr. Granite. "They have come from my home planet, Etinarg."

"Yes," said the first alien. "Everybody on Etinarg is named Mr. Granite. Etinarg is 'granite' spelled backward."

Wow! A whole planet filled with guys named Mr. Granite? That must get confusing. I guess when somebody on Etinarg calls out, "Hey, Mr. Granite!" everybody turns around.

"So all the men on your planet look exactly the same?" asked Ryan.

"Yes," said Mr. Granite, "and so do

all the women."

What?! Even the *women* look like Mr. Granite?

"In fact," said one of the alien Mr. Granites, "half of us *are* women."

Eeeeeeeeek! How do they tell the difference between men and women? I didn't want to know.

Our teacher Mr. Granite went over and hugged one of the alien Mr. Granites. Then all the other Mr. Granites went over to hug our Mr. Granite. Everybody was hugging everybody else.

"Mr. Granite!" said Mr. Granite.

"Mr. Granite!" said the alien who looked just like Mr. Granite.

"Mr. Granite!"

"Mr. Granite!"

"Mr. Granite!"

All the Mr. Granites were hugging each other and crying because they hadn't seen our Mr. Granite in so long. It was like

a meeting of Elvis impersonators, except they looked like Mr. Granite instead of Elvis.

"Did the earthlings harm you in any way?" one of the Mr. Granites asked our Mr. Granite.

"No," Mr. Granite told Mr. Granite. "These are my students, and they were good to me."

"On Earth, we're very well behaved," said Andrea, who's such a brownnoser that she'll even kiss up to aliens from other planets.

"What about the larger earthlings?" asked one of the Mr. Granites.

"They have been very kind to me," said

Mr. Granite. "The principal of the school even gave me a key to the teachers' lounge."

The teachers' lounge is a magical secret place where they have hot tubs, back rubs, and all the ice cream and candy you can eat.

"Are you going to take over the world and turn us into flesh-eating robots?" I asked one of the Mr. Granites.

I saw that in a movie once. It was cool.

"No," said all the Mr. Granites.

"Are you going to turn us into killer zombie robot slaves?" asked Michael.

"No," said all the Mr. Granites.

"Then why are you here?" asked Alexia.

"We have come to—"

The alien Mr. Granite didn't have the chance to finish his sentence, because at that very moment our principal, Mr. Klutz, came running out onto the playground.

He has no hair at all. I mean *none*. His head is so shiny, it squeaks.

"What's the meaning of this?" asked Mr. Klutz. "Is this some kind of a joke?"

No, a joke would be like . . .

Q: What's the difference between a guitar and a fish?

A: You can't tune a fish.

Get it? Tune a fish? Tuna fish? Anyway, the point is that Mr. Klutz totally doesn't know what a joke is.

"These men and women are from the planet Etinarg," Andrea told Mr. Klutz. "Their names are Mr. Granite."

"I figured that," said Mr. Klutz. "They all look just like our Mr. Granite. To what do we owe the pleasure of your company, Mr. Granites?"

That's grown-up talk for "What are *you* doing here?"

"We have a very important mission," said one of the alien Mr. Granites. "We have come to take your Mr. Granite home with us, to Etinarg."

WHAT?!

Saying Good-bye Is Sad

The alien Mr. Granites were going to take our Mr. Granite away! Everybody started yelling and screaming and freaking out.

"Noooooooooo!"

"Don't gooooooooo!"

As much as I hate to use the *L* word, we all love Mr. Granite. We didn't want him to leave.

"Mr. Granite has been teaching at our school for a long time," said Mr. Klutz to the aliens. "Why are you suddenly showing up *now*?"

Good question. That's why Mr. Klutz is the principal.

"We do apologize for our lateness," said one of the Mr. Granites. "Etinarg is a hundred million light-years away from Earth. It took us a long time to get here. And besides, we got stuck in traffic."

He was definitely lying about that. I don't even think they *have* traffic in outer space. Whenever my parents are late for anything, they always say they were stuck in traffic. That's the first rule of being a grown-up.

I wondered if the alien Mr. Granites were going to peel off their faces. Aliens are always peeling off their faces in the movies. That's the first rule of being an alien. And peeling off your face is cool. I wish I could peel off my face.

"Are you going to peel your faces off?" I

asked the Mr. Granites.

"Don't mind if I do," they all replied.

The alien Mr. Granites reached up to the tops of their heads with both hands. All the girls screamed. I covered my eyes with my hands. I wanted to see the Mr. Granites peel off their faces, but at the same time I didn't want to see what was underneath. What if it was scary? So I covered my eyes, but I opened my fingers so I could look between them.

All the Mr. Granites pulled at the top of their heads. The heads opened up like pistachio nuts. Then they peeled their entire faces off!

It was *awesome.* And you'll never believe

in a million hundred years what the Mr. Granites looked like underneath their faces.

They looked exactly the same!

"That was refreshing," said one of the Mr. Granites as he threw his old face off to the side.

"Hey!" Alexia said. "Those faces look just like the ones you peeled off!"

"It never hurts to have an extra face," said one of the Mr. Granites.

Even though the peeled-off faces looked exactly the same as their regular faces, it was still pretty cool. It's not every day you get to see a bunch of aliens peel their faces off.

All the Mr. Granites started hugging and crying again. It was hard to tell which of the Mr. Granites was ours because they all looked the same.

"I didn't think you would ever come for me," said our Mr. Granite.

"We never forgot about you, Mr. Granite,"

said one of the Mr. Granites.

"We heard that you built a spaceship," said another one of the Mr. Granites.

"Yes," said our Mr. Granite. "But a cow bumped into it when I was taking off. I almost died."

"That won't happen this time, Mr. Granite," said one of the other Mr. Granites. "We must leave now, before any more cows come around."

Everybody started yelling and sobbing and freaking out.

"Don't leave us, Mr. Granite!" begged Alexia.

"Please please please *please*!" we all begged.

Saying "please" over and over and over

again usually works with grown-ups. At least, *human* grown-ups.

"I have enjoyed my time on Earth as your third-grade teacher," said Mr. Granite. "But Etinarg is my home. Now I must return to my own planet."

Everybody was moaning and groaning and freaking out.

"Mr. Klutz, can't you *do* something?" asked Emily. "You're the principal!"

"Yeah!" we all said.

Mr. Klutz held up his hand and made a peace sign, which means "shut up." Then he took a step forward to shake Mr. Granite's hand.

"You are a great teacher, Mr. Granite," he said. "We will miss you here at Ella

Mentry School."

"I'm not a teacher," said Mr. Granite. "You must mean the *other* Mr. Granite."

"Oh yes," said Mr. Klutz. "I'm sorry. It's very confusing when you all look alike."

"No worries," said all the Mr. Granites. They started moving up the ramp to go back inside their spaceship.

The Mr. Granite who was our teacher went over to Mr. Klutz and they hugged.

"We borrowed Mr. Granite from the good people of Etinarg," Mr. Klutz told us. "But now we must return him. When you borrow something, you should always return it."

"I really enjoyed working at Ella Mentry

School," Mr. Granite said. "Leaving here makes me feel sad."

Everybody was choked up. Even Mr. Klutz looked like he was going to cry.

Mr. Granite gathered all the kids in our class around him for a group hug.

"I'm going to miss you kids more than anything else," he said, tears in his eyes.

"We're going to miss you too, Mr. Granite," we all said.

"When I get home," said Mr. Granite, "I'm going to name my Etinarg friends A.J., Andrea, Ryan, Emily, Michael, Alexia, and Neil."

We were all sobbing and blubbering and blowing our noses into tissues.

Well, only one nose per person. It would be weird to blow two noses.

"I hope you kids will remember what I told you this year," said Mr. Granite.

I thought back and remembered some of the things Mr. Granite had told me during the year. . . .

I *before* E *except after* C. *Sit down. Be*

quiet. Stop talking. Tie your sneakers. Stop bothering Andrea. Stop talking. Stop picking your nose. No, you can't go to the boys' room now. Where's your homework? Stop talking. Go to the principal's office. Stop making armpit farts. . . .

Ah, those were the good old days.

Mr. Granite pulled himself away from us and climbed into the spaceship with all the other Mr. Granites. The ramp slid up into the ship. A few minutes later, the countdown began . . .

10 . . . 9 . . . 8 . . .

Dark smoke started coming out of the spaceship.

7 . . . 6 . . . 5 . . .

I could hear that weird humming sound.

4 . . . 3 . . . 2 . . .

Colored lights started flashing.

1 . . .

Just before the spaceship was about to take off, a window opened up. Mr. Granite poked his head out of the window and shouted to us.

"Turn to page twenty-three in your math books . . ."

But he never had the chance to finish his sentence.*

---

*Hey, how come this book is called *Mr. Cooper Is Super!* There hasn't been anybody named Mr. Cooper in it. That's weird.

The New Teacher

We all watched as the spaceship with Mr. Granite inside lifted slowly up off the playground. This time there were no cows around to mess things up. The ship zoomed to the left. Then it zipped to the right. And then it was gone.

Mr. Granite had left the planet.

For a few seconds nobody said anything. There was nothing to say.

Then Emily the crybaby started cry-ing, of course. After that *everybody* was crying. Even me. Mr. Granite was weird, but he was a really good teacher.

"What are we going to do *now*?" Andrea asked, wiping her eyes. "We don't have a teacher anymore. How can we learn anything without a teacher?"

That's when I got the greatest idea in the history of the world. If Mr. Granite was gone, we didn't have a teacher. And if we didn't have a teacher, we couldn't learn anything. And if we couldn't learn anything, there was no point in going to school. And if there was no point in going to school, they would have to shut it down!

"No more school!" I shouted, jumping up and down. "No more school! No more school!"

I figured *everybody* was going to jump

up and down chanting "No more school!" with me.

I looked around. Nobody else was jumping up and down. Nobody else was chanting. Everybody was looking at me.

I hate when that happens. I stopped chanting.

"We'll just have to deal with this tomorrow," said Mr. Klutz sadly. "For now, let's all go home. It's three o'clock. Time for dismissal."

The next morning I couldn't wait to get to school and find out who our new teacher would be. Was it going to be a man or a lady? Young or old? Dark hair or blond hair? Short or tall? Skinny or fat? Human or robot? Meat eater or plant eater? Regular or extra crispy?

As it turned out, the answer was "none of the above." When I got to our class-room, there was no teacher in there at all! So me and Michael and Ryan did what we always do when there are no grown-ups around. We shook our butts at the class.

"Boys!" Andrea said, rolling her eyes.

"I wonder who our new teacher is going to be," said Alexia.

"Beats me," said Neil the nude kid.

"Where would you go to get a new teacher anyway?" asked Ryan.

"Rent-A-Teacher," I replied. "You can rent anything."

"We'll probably have a substitute teacher for a few days," said Andrea, who thinks she knows everything. "Mr. Klutz will need a little time to hire a new teacher."

"Teachers get hired?" I asked. "Does that mean they get paid, too?"

"Of *course* teachers get paid, dumbhead!" said Andrea.

I wanted to say something mean to Andrea, but I couldn't come up with anything besides "So is your face!"

I didn't know that teachers got paid. I thought they just came to school every day because they had nowhere else to go.

"Maybe Miss Daisy will become our teacher again," said Emily, all excited.

Miss Daisy was our teacher in second grade. She was a good teacher, except for the fact that she couldn't read, write, or do math.

Come to think of it, she was the dumbest teacher in the history of the world.

"Her name isn't Miss Daisy anymore," Andrea said. "She got married, so now her name is *Mrs.* Daisy."

When ladies get married, they go from "Miss" to "Mrs." And sometimes they go from "Miss" to "Ms." Nobody knows why.

But our new teacher wasn't going to be Miss Daisy. And it wasn't going to be Mrs. Daisy. And it wasn't going to be Ms. Daisy either. Because the most amazing thing in the history of the world happened. You'll never believe who ran into the door at that moment.

It was a guy wearing a superhero costume! He ran right into the door! Then he fell into the classroom, slammed into the teacher's desk, and toppled over onto the floor.

"Owww!" the guy moaned. "I think I may have broken my leg!"

We all ran to the front of the class to help the guy up.

"Are you Superman?" Alexia asked.

"No," he replied. "I am *Cooper Man*!"

Mr. Cooper Is Super!

Cooper Man told us to sit in our seats. I guess his leg wasn't broken after all, because he limped and hobbled over to the whiteboard. He wrote this on it, in big letters. . . .

MR. COOPER

"Are you a real superhero?" asked Ryan.

"Of course I am!" Mr. Cooper said. "Can't you see my cape?"

Superheroes always wear capes. Nobody knows why. You never see regular people walking down the street wearing a cape. What's up with that? Capes are cool.

At that point Mr. Klutz came into the classroom.

"Ah, Mr. Cooper! I'm so glad you were able to find your room. I was going to introduce you to the children, but it looks like you've already done that. Kids, Mr. Cooper will be your new teacher. From now on, you are under his supervision."

"Wow, Mr. Cooper has super vision!" I shouted. "Can you see through walls?"

"Of course," Mr. Cooper said. "Especially walls that have windows in them."

"I have to go to a meeting," Mr. Klutz told Mr. Cooper. "I'll stop back here later to see how you're making out."

"Ewwwww, gross!" Everybody started choking and gagging because Mr. Klutz said "making out."

As soon as Mr. Klutz left, Mr. Cooper picked up a math book from Mr. Granite's desk.

Oh no! It looked like he was going to teach us math! I thought that after Mr. Granite was gone, we would never have to learn math again.

Bummer in the summer!

If a grown-up is about to say something you don't want to hear, you should change the subject as soon as possible. That's the first rule of being a kid. But I didn't know what to say. I didn't know what to do. I had to think fast.

"Do you have real superpowers?" I asked Mr. Cooper.

"Of course I do," he replied. "I wouldn't be much of a superhero if I didn't have superpowers."

"Can you fly?" asked Andrea.

"Sure I can fly," said Mr. Cooper.

"Oooooh, show us!" everybody started shouting.

"I only fly on Wednesdays," said Mr. Cooper. "And today is Thursday."

"Can you be invisible?" asked Alexia.

"Of course."

"Prove it!" we all shouted.

"I already did," said Mr. Cooper. "Before I came in the door, you didn't see me, did you?"

"No."

"That's because I was invisible."

"He's right!" I shouted.

"Do you have superstrength?" asked Ryan. "Can you bend steel bars with your bare hands?"

"That's easy-peasy," said Mr. Cooper, "but I wouldn't want to ruin a perfectly good steel bar."

"Do you have heat vision?" asked Michael. "Can you burn things up just by looking at them?"

"Of course," said Mr. Cooper. "But why would anybody want to do that?"

"It would be a cool way to cook hot dogs," I said. "Or you could toast marshmallows with your eyes."

"Hmmm, I never thought of that," said Mr. Cooper. "But I will show you another superpower I have. I can make you think of anything I want you to think about."

"What?" we all said. "No way!"

"You can't do that!" said Neil.

"Nobody tells *me* what to think about!" said Alexia.

"Fine," said Mr. Cooper. "*Don't* think of an enormous pink elephant, right here in this classroom."

"Okay, I won't," I said.

"And this enormous pink elephant is wearing a tutu," said Mr. Cooper.

Everybody laughed. It would be funny to see an enormous pink elephant wearing a tutu.

"And the elephant is holding a little umbrella, and it's singing 'John Jacob Jingleheimer Schmidt,'" said Mr. Cooper. "I can make you think about that in your head."

I tried not to think about an enormous pink elephant wearing a tutu and holding a little umbrella while it's singing "John Jacob Jingleheimer Schmidt."

But it was impossible! In fact, *all* I could think about was an enormous pink

elephant wearing a tutu and holding a little umbrella while it's singing "John Jacob
Jingleheimer Schmidt"!

"I'm thinking about it!" said Andrea. "I
can picture it in my head!"

"Me too!" said Emily. "I can't help it!"

The whole class was thinking about
an enormous pink elephant wearing a
tutu and holding a little umbrella while
it's singing "John Jacob Jingleheimer
Schmidt"!*

"He did it!" shouted Michael. "Mr. Cooper can make people think of anything he
wants!"

"It's amazing!" said Alexia.

---

*And so are you, I bet.

"See?" said Mr. Cooper. "I told you I had superpowers."

"He really *is* a superhero!" said Ryan. "Mr. Cooper is super!"

If you ask me, Mr. Cooper is weird.

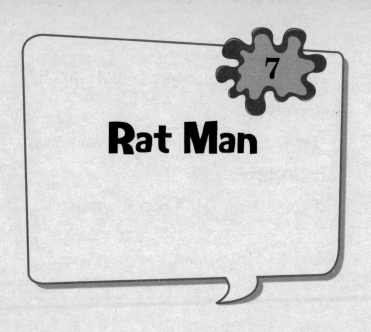

Rat Man

We were all thinking about enormous pink elephants wearing tutus, holding little umbrellas, and singing "John Jacob Jingleheimer Schmidt." Mr. Cooper told us he would be back in a minute, and he stepped out of the room. Me and Michael and Ryan got up and shook our butts at the class. Everybody laughed except for

Andrea and Emily, who just rolled their eyes.

A minute later Mr. Cooper came running back into the room. This time he almost knocked over the computer in the corner and fell down again. Man, for a superhero, Mr. Cooper falls down a lot.

He was wearing a different costume this time. There was a big *R* on his cape. He also had a wedge of cheese hanging off his belt. That was weird.

"Behold!" he announced. "I am Rat Man!"

"Rat Man?" I said. "I thought you were Cooper Man."

"That must have been some other guy," said Mr. Cooper. "I am Rat Man, and I have come to teach you about rats."

WHAT?!

"Rats? Why do we have to learn about rats?" Andrea asked. "I think rats are disgusting!"

"No they're not," said Mr. Cooper as he stepped into the hallway and came back with a big cage in his hand. "Rats are fascinating animals."

"Eeeeeeeek!" screamed all the girls, except for Alexia. "He has live rats! Gross!"

"Cool!" yelled all the boys and Alexia.

"Male rats are called bucks," Mr. Cooper said as he took one of the rats out of the cage and petted it. "Females are called does, and babies are called kittens or pups. But I call this one Wilbur."

The girls were freaking out, but Wilbur
didn't seem all that scary to me. Mr. Cooper told us that rats are smart, friendly,
and social. When a rat gets sick, its rat
friends will even take care of it. He told us
lots of other neat stuff about rats, too.

"Do you want to pet Wilbur?" asked Mr. Cooper.

"No!" shouted all the girls.

"Yes!" shouted all the boys.

"Oh, come on," said Mr. Cooper. "I bet at least *one* of the girls must be brave enough to pet Wilbur."

"I'll do it!" said Little Miss Perfect, who will do anything to impress a teacher.

Andrea scrunched up her eyes, and Mr. Cooper carefully put Wilbur in her hands.

"See? Wilbur really likes you," said Mr. Cooper.

That's when the most amazing thing in the history of the world happened. Andrea must have twitched or something, because Wilbur jumped off her hand, landed on the floor, and ran away.

"Eeeeeeek!" everybody shrieked.

Wilbur ran toward the back of the room.

"Calm down, everyone," said Mr. Cooper. "Please calm down!"

"There's a loose rat in the class!"

"Run for your lives!"

We were all freaking out. It was just a rat. What's the big deal?

"I'll get him!" said Andrea.

Everybody was running around like the earth had been hit by an asteroid or something. Half the class was chasing Wilbur, and the other half of the class was running away from him.

Finally, Andrea and I cornered Wilbur in the corner.* Wilbur looked at Andrea. Wilbur looked at me.

"Put your lunch box over him, Arlo," said Andrea. She calls me by my real name because she knows I don't like it.

"I'm not putting my lunch box over a *rat*!" I told her. "Why don't you put *your* lunch box over him?"

"I don't *have* my lunch box today," Andrea said. "I'm buying lunch in the vomitorium."

"Well, use your pencil case!" I told Andrea.

---

*If you're going to corner something, it should be in a corner. That's the first rule of cornering stuff.

"I'm not putting my pencil case over a rat!" she replied. "Why don't you use *your* pencil case?"

We went back and forth like that for a while. Wilbur was still cornered in the corner. He looked nervous.

And you'll never believe who walked into the door at that moment.

Nobody! It would hurt if you walked into a door. But you'll never believe who walked into the door*way*.

It was Mr. Klutz!

"How are you kids making out?" he asked.

"Ewwwww, gross!" Everybody started choking and gagging because Mr. Klutz said "making out" again.

"We're learning about rats," said Mr. Cooper. "But one of them seems to have escaped."

"You brought live rats to school with you?" asked Mr. Klutz. "Are you out of your mind, Mr. Cooper? Is this any way to teach the children?"

"Sure it is," Mr. Cooper replied. "See? A.J. and Andrea are totally engaged."

"Ooooo!" Ryan said. "A.J. and Andrea are *engaged*!"

"When are you two gonna get *married*?" asked Michael.

If those guys weren't my best friends, I would hate them.

The Attack of Super Librarian

After a million hundred hours, we were able to capture Wilbur the rat and get him back inside his cage.

"Okay, it's time for math," said Rat Man, I mean Mr. Cooper.

Noooooooooo! Not math! Anything but math! Why do we have to learn math?

Isn't that why they invented calculators?

"I love math!" said Andrea. "Math is fun!"

What is her problem? Why can't a truck full of math books fall on her head?

I wanted to go to Antarctica and live with the penguins. This was the worst thing to happen since TV Turnoff Week.

"Turn to page twenty-three in your books," said Mr. Cooper. "Does anybody have any questions?"

"I do," I said. "How old are rocks? Who was the first person to drink milk from a cow? Why don't we have fall and spring Olympics? Who invented sandpaper? What color is the White House?"

"*Math* questions, A.J.," said Mr. Cooper. "Do you have any questions about *math*?"

"Yes," I said. "Why do we have to learn math?"

Mr. Cooper looked mad. I think he was going to say something mean to me, but he never got the chance. Because you'll never believe who ran into the door at that moment.

Nobody! You'd have to be crazy to run into a door. I thought we went over that already. But you'll never believe who ran into the door*way*.

It was a *lady* dressed up in a superhero costume! She had a big *L* on her cape. She was wearing a mask over her eyes, but she looked a lot like our librarian, Mrs. Roopy.

"Oh no!" shouted Mr. Cooper. "My arch-enemy is here!"

"What do you have against arches?" I asked.

Everybody laughed even though I didn't say anything funny.

"It is I," announced the lady as she struck a superhero pose, "Super Librarian!"

"You look a lot like Mrs. Roopy," said Andrea.

"Roopy?" asked the masked lady. "Never heard of her. I am Super Librarian!"

She *really* looked a lot like Mrs. Roopy to me.

"Oh, yeah? What superpowers do *you* have?" asked Alexia.

"I can log in books and check them out at superspeed," said Super Librarian. "And I have memorized the entire Dewey decimal system. Pick a number, and I will tell you what books go with that number."

"Number 796," shouted Ryan.

"You will find books about sports in 796," replied Super Librarian.

"She's right!" shouted Ryan. "She really

does have superpowers!"

"She does not," said Neil the nude kid. "I bet lots of librarians know the Dewey decimal system."

"Well, I can leap over a giant stack of books in a single bound," said Super Librarian.

"That's not such a big deal," said Michael.

"Oh, yeah?" said Super Librarian. "Well, I can shelve books with one hand!"

"No way!" we all shouted.

It's *impossible* to shelve a book with one hand. You need one hand to move the other books aside and your second hand to slip the book into its place.

"Watch *this*!" said Super Librarian.

She went over to the bookcase and

put one hand behind her back. Then she pulled out a book from the shelf and slipped it between the books on another shelf using just one hand.

"WOW," everybody said, which is "MOM" upside down.

"Your powers are indeed strong, Super Librarian," said Mr. Cooper. "But why are you here?"

"I have come to get your overdue library books," said Super Librarian.

"I don't have any overdue library books," said Mr. Cooper.

"Oh no?" said Super Librarian as she ran back to the bookcase, pulled out a book, and waved it in the air. "Then what's *this*?"

"That's a . . . I mean . . . uh . . ."

"It's overdue!" shouted Super Librarian. "If you borrow something, it's important to return it. So now you must pay for your crimes against humanity!"

"B-b-but . . . I just . . . started working here. . . ."

"No buts!" shouted Super Librarian.

Everybody started giggling because Super Librarian said "buts," which sounds just like "butts" even though it only has one *t*.

I thought she was going to make Mr. Cooper pay a fine for his overdue library book. But that's not what happened at all. Instead, the weirdest thing in the history of the world happened.

The two of them started fighting!

Mr. Cooper and Super Librarian squared off and began to do karate chops and kicks at each other. It was cool.

"Ooooof!" yelled Mr. Cooper.

"Take *that*!" yelled Super Librarian. "And that!"

Everybody was yelling and screaming and hooting and hollering.

"Man, that lady is *really* serious about overdue library books," said Ryan.

Mr. Cooper did one of those spinning leg kicks, but Super Librarian blocked it, and he fell on the floor. It was exciting! We were all glued to our seats.

Well, not really. Why would anybody glue themselves to a seat? That would be weird. How would you get the glue off?

"I don't approve of all this violence," said Andrea. "It sets a bad example for children."

"What do you have against violins?" I asked.

"Not violins, Arlo!" said Andrea. "Violence! I don't approve of *violence*!"

"Can you possibly be more boring?" I asked.

After a few more vicious karate chops and kicks, Mr. Cooper fell down again. Super Librarian jumped on top of him and pinned him to the floor.

"Say uncle!" shouted Super Librarian.

"Uncle," groaned Mr. Cooper.*

---

*When you lose a fight, you have to say "uncle." Nobody knows why.

Super Librarian got up off Mr. Cooper and helped him stand up.

"I'll take this book back to the library, where it belongs," said Super Librarian.

"I'm sorry it was overdue," said Mr. Cooper.

"I accept your apology," said Super Librarian. "See that it doesn't happen again. And I hope you kids will be sure to always return your books to the library. If you don't, you will face the wrath of . . . Super Librarian!"

Then she picked up the overdue book and dashed out of the room.

Mrs. Roopy is loopy.

9

The Truth about Mr. Cooper

We were in the vomitorium eating lunch. I had a peanut butter and jelly sandwich. Michael had a peanut butter and jelly sandwich. Neil and Alexia had peanut butter and jelly sandwiches. In case you were wondering, we *all* had peanut butter and jelly sandwiches.

Well, everyone except Ryan. He had a jelly and peanut butter sandwich. He likes to do things backward. One time Ryan invented the wichsand, which is a sand-wich with the stuff on the outside and the bread in the middle.

"Mr. Cooper is weird," I said to the gang. "He's always falling down and tripping over his own feet."

"He's kind of a doofus," said Ryan.

We all laughed, because "doofus" is a funny word. It's hard to say "doofus" with-out laughing.

"Yeah, superheroes aren't supposed to fall down so much," said Alexia.

"Shhhhhh!" whispered Neil. "Mr. Cooper

might hear you."

"How could he possibly hear us?" asked Michael.

"Maybe he has superhearing," whispered Neil. "He told us he can make himself invisible. He may be standing behind us right *now*!"

We all turned around. Mr. Cooper wasn't there. Just to be on the safe side, I took out a pen and wrote a secret message on my napkin. . . .

MAYBE MR. COOPER ISN'T A REAL TEACHER.

I showed my napkin to the gang. They all grabbed pens and started writing secret messages on their napkins. . . .

Alexia: MAYBE HE LOCKED OUR REAL TEACHER IN AN ABANDONED BARN!

Ryan: AND HE'S GOING TO SET IT ON FIRE!

Michael: I SAW THAT IN A MOVIE ONCE.

Neil: STUFF LIKE THAT HAPPENS ALL THE TIME.

Me: FIRE IS COOL.

At the next table, Andrea and Emily were looking over at us.

"What are you doing?" Andrea asked.

"We're writing secret messages," I told her, "so Mr. Cooper can't use his super-hearing to listen to what we're saying."

"Oh." Andrea sat back down. She had on her worried face, like she was expecting an asteroid to strike the earth or something.

"What's bugging you?" I asked her. "Did you get an A minus on something?"

"I'm worried about Mr. Cooper," Andrea replied.

"What about him?"

"My mom is a psychologist," Andrea said, "and she told me that when people dress up in costumes all the time, it's because they're sad and lonely and don't like their own lives."

"What? That's crazy!" I said. "Maybe Mr. Cooper just likes dressing up in superhero costumes."

"Or maybe he really *is* a superhero," said Alexia.

"Or maybe he's just sad and lonely and he needs a hug," said Emily.

"Well, how are we going to find out which it is?" asked Neil the nude kid.

That's when I came up with the greatest idea in the history of the world.

"Let's go sneak around and spy on him!" I suggested.

"Yeah!" everybody agreed. Even Andrea and Emily.

Spying on people is cool. We cleaned off our trays and sneaked out of the vomitorium. Then we sneaked down the hallway. Then we sneaked over to our classroom.

I was the first one to peek inside. I saw Mr. Cooper through the little window in the door.

"He's in there!" I told the gang.

"Shhhhh!" Everybody shushed me.

"What's he doing?" asked Andrea.

"It looks like he's eating a sandwich," I reported.

"What kind of sandwich?" asked Ryan, who is really into sandwiches.

"Who *cares* what kind of sandwich he's eating?" asked Alexia.

"It could be important," said Ryan.

"It doesn't matter what kind of a

sandwich he's eating," said Michael.

"It does too."

"It does not."

We went back and forth like that for a while. As we were arguing, the door suddenly opened and Mr. Cooper came out.

"What are you kids doing here?" he asked. "Shouldn't you be eating in the lunchroom?"

I didn't know what to say. I didn't know what to do. I had to think fast.

"Aha!" I said. "We *caught* you!"

"Caught me doing what?" asked Mr. Cooper.

"We caught you eating a sandwich!" I said.

"Superheroes need to eat too," said Mr.

Cooper. "We need to keep up our super-strength."

"Why don't you eat in the teachers' lounge?" asked Neil.

"Yeah," said Alexia. "Why don't you eat in the teachers' lounge?"

"The door was locked," Mr. Cooper told us. "Mr. Klutz didn't give me a key yet."

"Why don't you use your superstrength to kick down the door to the teachers' lounge?" asked Ryan.

"Yeah!" said Michael. "If you were a *real* superhero, you would kick down the door."

Michael had a point. Besides, kicking down doors is cool. On cop shows, they

never use the doorknob to open a door.
They just kick it down. What's up with
that? When cops are at home with their
families, do they kick down the doors
whenever they enter a room? I tried to
kick down a door once, but I hurt my foot.

"If I kicked down the door to the teachers' lounge, we'd have to get a new door,"
said Mr. Cooper.

Hmmm. He was right about that.

"Do you need a hug?" Andrea asked Mr.
Cooper.

"I can *always* use a hug," he replied.
"Will you give me a superhug?"

We all gave Mr. Cooper a big group hug.
But I still didn't trust him. He always has

some excuse for not using his superpowers. I was beginning to think that maybe
Mr. Cooper wasn't a superhero after all.

Maybe, for a change, Andrea was right.

The Big Surprise Ending!

10

The next morning Mr. Cooper came running into our classroom. He told us he was Lava Man, and he taught us all about volcanoes. Then he ran out of the room and came back as Weather Man. He taught us all about meteorology. Then he ran out of the room and came back as Electric Man.

He taught us all about electricity. It's fun to learn stuff from a superhero, whether he's a real superhero or not.

At recess Mr. Cooper and Mrs. Roopy were the teachers on duty. We were all on the swings, minding our own business, when the weirdest thing in the history of the world happened.

"Look! Up in the sky!" yelled Andrea.

"It's a bird!" yelled Emily.

"It's a plane!" yelled Alexia.

"No, it's a spaceship!" yelled Ryan.

Ryan was right! It *was* a spaceship. In fact, it looked just like the Mr. Granites' spaceship. And it was coming down right over the playground!

"The Mr. Granites are back!" shouted Michael.

"I'm scared," said Emily, who is scared of everything.

"They're going to take over the world and turn us into flesh-eating robots!" I shouted.

"They're going to turn us into killer zombie robot slaves!" shouted Michael.

"Run for your lives!" shouted Neil the nude kid.

Everybody was freaking out. What could the Mr. Granites possibly want *this* time?

"If only there was a real superhero to save us!" said Andrea.

Andrea looked at Mr. Cooper. Ryan looked at Mr. Cooper. Michael looked at Mr. Cooper. Alexia looked at Mr. Cooper.

In case you were wondering, *everybody* was looking at Mr. Cooper.

"Leave it to me," Mr. Cooper announced, taking a step forward. "I am . . . Cooper Man!"

Oh no, I thought. We're done for.

Smoke poured out of the spaceship. Colored lights were flashing. There was a weird humming sound.

The spaceship touched down in the middle of the playground. All the smoke and lights and humming stopped. Then the ramp slid down from the bottom of the spaceship.

"Stand back, everyone," said Mr. Cooper. "I'll handle this."

Mr. Cooper walked over to the end of the ramp.

The door to the spaceship opened.

We were all on pins and needles.

Well, not really. We were standing up. If we were on pins and needles, it would have hurt.

But you should have been there! Electricity was in the air.

Well, not exactly. If there was electricity in the air, all of us would have been electrocuted.

But it was really exciting!

Mr. Granite came out of the spaceship and down the ramp. Well, I *think* it was Mr. Granite. It could have been one of the other Mr. Granites. It could have been *anybody* from the planet Etinarg. They all look alike.

In any case, one of those creatures that looked just like Mr. Granite came down the ramp.

"Greetings, earthling," said the Mr. Granite look-alike. "Who are you?"

"I am the new third-grade teacher at Ella Mentry School," said Mr. Cooper. "Did you come back to destroy the earth?"

"No."

"Did you come back to take over the world and turn us into flesh-eating robots?" asked Mr. Cooper.

"No."

"Did you come to turn us into killer zombie robot slaves?" Mr. Cooper asked.

"No."

"Then why did you come back to Earth?"

"When I left the other day," said Mr. Granite, "I forgot to give back my key to the teachers' lounge. When you borrow something, you should always return it."

"Like library books!" yelled Mrs. Roopy.

Wow! Mr. Granite traveled a million hundred light-years just to bring back the key to the teachers' lounge! That was weird.

Mr. Granite handed Mr. Cooper the key.

"Thank you," said Mr. Cooper. "Now I don't have to eat my lunch in the class-room anymore."

Mr. Granite turned around and went back up the ramp into the spaceship. The door closed behind him. We all breathed a sigh of relief.

I felt like this called for a celebration.

"Mr. Cooper saved the earth!" I shouted, jumping up and down. "Hooray for Mr. Cooper! Hooray for Mr. Cooper! Hooray for Mr. Cooper!"

I figured everybody was going to jump up and down chanting "Hooray for Mr.

Cooper!" with me.

I looked around. Nobody else was jumping up and down. Nobody else was chanting. Everybody was looking at me.

I hate when that happens. I stopped chanting.

Smoke poured out of the spaceship. Colored lights were flashing. There was a weird humming sound. Then the window of the spaceship opened.

"Good-bye again!" Mr. Granite yelled out to us.

"Good-bye, Mr. Granite!" we all yelled.

10 . . . 9 . . . 8 . . . 7 . . . 6 . . . 5 . . . 4 . . . 3 . . . 2 . . . 1 . . .

The spaceship lifted off. It zoomed to

the left. It zipped to the right. And then it was gone forever.

Well, that's pretty much what happened. Maybe another spaceship will land in the playground someday. Maybe Mr. Granite will grow some hair out of his ears. Maybe cops will start using the doorknob instead of kicking down doors all the time. Maybe they'll come up with some different names for the people who live on planet Etinarg. Maybe the aliens will come back and turn us into flesh-eating robots. Maybe Mr. Klutz will learn what a joke is. Maybe grown-ups will stop saying they're stuck in traffic all the time. Maybe cows will stop bumping into spaceships. Maybe regular people will start wearing capes. Maybe aliens will stop peeling their faces off all the time. Maybe Mr. Cooper will use his heat vision to cook hot dogs with his eyes. Maybe a pink elephant wearing a tutu will come into our classroom and sing "John Jacob Jingleheimer Schmidt." Maybe Wilbur the rat will come visit our class again. Maybe Mrs. Roopy will admit that she's really Super Librarian. Maybe Andrea will stop complaining about violins. Maybe our real teacher will escape from the burning barn. Maybe I will give back Michael's football. Maybe Mr. Cooper will stop running into doors, falling down, and being such a doofus.

But it won't be easy!